SWEET DREAMS

Sharing Sweet Dreams

Bedtime for little ones isn't always as peaceful as we would like! Yet it can also be a warm and loving time, when confidences are shared, the troubles and excitements of the day are resolved, and little ones fall asleep with a contentment that we can only envy.

We all know that a bedtime routine helps, and a bedtime story can be an enjoyable part of that routine for everyone. But some stories are far from soothing. *Sweet Dreams* has been specially written with peaceful bedtimes in mind.

The stories are really short, a perfect just-before-bedtime length, and most give lots of opportunities to talk with your child about his or her own experiences and share your own feelings, too.

Each story touches on a different issue—the kinds of happy and difficult emotions most children feel. You can consult the index of themes on page 80 for help in choosing an appropriate story. As each one is short, skim through it yourself first to make sure it is what you need.

Wishing you happy (and peaceful) bedtimes!   *NMAB*

SWEET DREAMS

Written by *Nicola Baxter*

Illustrated by *Pauline Siewert*

BACK**PACK**BOOKS
·
NEW YORK

Wishing special sweet dreams to
Joshua, Poppy, Emma, Milly, Lottie, Kizzy, and Shane

This 2005 edition published
by Backpack Books,
by arrangement with Armadillo Books,
an imprint of Bookmart Ltd.

2005 Backpack Books

ISBN-13: 978-0-7607-7184-6
ISBN-10: 0-7607-7184-7

Printed and bound in China

First published by Amradillo Books, an imprint of
Bookmart Limited

Produced for Bookmart Limited by Nicola Baxter

Designer: Amanda Hawkes
Production designer: Amy Barton
Editorial consultant: Sara Morling

3 5 7 9 10 8 6 4 2

Contents

The Bad Day

Once there was a little boy who had a very bad day. He didn't mean to be nasty, but somehow it just happened.

By the end of the day, everyone was grumpy. The little boy was grumpy, too. He climbed into bed and clenched his fists tight. He wanted to shout and cry.

Then someone who loved him very much sat down by the side of his bed and told him,

"When you make a mess, *I love you.*

When you are cross, *I love you*. When you are sad, *I love you*. When you break things, *I love you*. When you slam the door and stamp your feet, *I love you*.

I love you all day and all night.

I love you with my head and my heart and my elbows! *I love all of you*, from your funny messy hair to your funny smelly feet. And I wouldn't know what to do without you."

Then the boy lay very still, and he felt all the bad feelings slowly, slowly trickling out of his toes! And oozing out of his ears! And floating out of his fingers! And each time he breathed out, they flew out of his nose! At last, there were no bad feelings left. There was just a warm, safe feeling, like a smile inside.

"I love you, too," he said.
And the smile became a grin.
And the grin became a laugh.
And the laugh cuddled him all
night long, until it was time to
wake up to a very *good* day.

7

The Dream

Once upon a time there was a dream. It was a beautiful dream. Sometimes it was pink and orange and blue. Sometimes it was purple and red and yellow. Sometimes it was the whole rainbow—all at once!

The dream floated along, looking for someone to share its secrets. Tucked away safely inside the dream there were all kinds of wonderful things. There were stars and seashells, flowers and ice cream, rainbows and ribbons, butterflies and buses. In fact, there was everything you like best in the whole world.

Here and there the dream floated. It seemed to know which way to go. Towards the end of the day, it floated towards a window. Like magic, it flew right through the window, into the room inside.

And what did the dream find?
It found a very special person,
snuggled up in bed and
listening to a story. A story like
this one. And the dream waited,
gently bobbing up and down,
just out of sight. It waited.

When the beautiful bright eyes of the very special person
were sleepy, the dream gave a happy little sigh—and
disappeared!

*Close your eyes now, gently, gently. Wait just
a moment and you will find the dream, as
beautiful as ever, safe inside you. And before
morning comes, it will show you wonderful things.*

Monsters *(you know where!)*

*There were once some monsters who lived under a little girl's bed. She didn't know they were there for a long time. Then, one day, they popped into her head, and she was **sure** they were there. But she didn't dare to look.*

"I cannot go to sleep with monsters under the bed," said the little girl. "No way."

The people she loved tried to help. They peered under the bed.

"There are no monsters there at all," said one. "Go to sleep."

"Not a monster to be seen," said another. "But I have found a smelly sock."

"That is not at all the kind of place a monster likes to live," they agreed.

But the little girl could not, would not go to sleep.
"Not while there are monsters under the bed," she said,
though she was very, very sleepy and her eyes kept closing.

Then, when everyone had gone, the door slowly, slowly
opened. In came a *big* monster! The little girl was so
surprised that she wasn't even afraid.

The monster marched straight up to the bed
and peered under it. "Come out, you naughty
monsterlings!" she cried. "It's time you were
tucked up in your monster beds. Come out
this minute, and don't let me *ever*
find you there again!"

So one, two, three, little monsters
crept out and followed their monster
mother out of the room.

The little girl said to herself,
"I knew I was right." She smiled,
and she snuggled,
and she slept.

*If you have a you-know-what you-know-where,
just close your eyes, for monster mothers can
be shy. But they will solve your problem
in a second, every time.*

The Dark

*T*here was once a boy called Fred who was afraid of the dark.

One night Grandpa put Fred to bed.
"Good night, Fred. Sweet dreams!" he said.
He switched off the light and turned to go,
But Fred sat up. He shouted, "No!"

"Don't touch that light! It must stay on!
I don't like the dark when you are gone."
Grandpa frowned. He scratched his head.
"You'd better tell me the problem, Fred."

"In the light," replied Fred, "all my things are there.
I can see my bed, and my desk, and my chair.
But when it's dark, I can't see my bed,
And there's . . . er . . . something scary there instead."

"What kind of a something?" Grandpa frowned.
"Don't say there are horrible monsters around?"
"Monsters!" laughed Fred. "No! They're all right.
It's a scary fairy who comes every night."

"A scary fairy?" said Grandpa. "That's rare.
Where is that scary fairy, where?"
"Sometimes on my bed. Sometimes on my chair."
Fred looked worried. "She's everywhere!"

But Grandpa had met scary fairies before.
He smiled as he stood by the bedroom door.
"She's not on your chair and not on your bed,
That scary fairy is inside your head!
Send her away! She'll do what you say.
Think of a friendly fairy instead!"

Fred shut his eyes. It was dark, but not scary,
For there on his chair was a friendly fairy!
Now she looks after him every night,
And Fred is happy to turn off the light.

A Perfect Night

Once upon a time there was a perfect starry sky. Its thousands of stars glittered and shimmered. Night after night, they danced— very, very slowly—through the dark.

Under the stars, there was a moon. It shone, white and perfect, in the starry sky. Sometimes it showed a full, round face. Sometimes just a tiny sliver of silver could be seen. Each night it slid silently across the sky beneath the stars.

Below the moon, there was a planet. It was blue and green, like a perfect sparkling jewel. All night it turned, gently spinning, under the moon, beneath the stars.

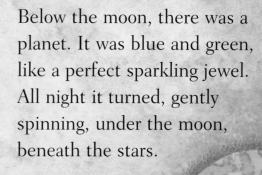

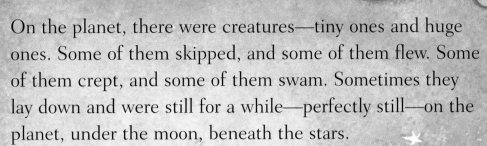

On the planet, there were creatures—tiny ones and huge ones. Some of them skipped, and some of them flew. Some of them crept, and some of them swam. Sometimes they lay down and were still for a while—perfectly still—on the planet, under the moon, beneath the stars.

Among the creatures, there was a person. A little person, safe in a soft, snuggly bed. And someone who loved the little person was always near. Because that little person was perfect, too, and very, very precious. The little person slept, breathing gently, dreaming and smiling, in the warm bed, on the planet, under the moon, beneath the stars.

And all night, the stars danced, and the moon slid, and the planet turned, and the little person slept, and everything was just as it should be.
Perfect.

The New Baby

Jake had a new baby sister. She was a happy baby. And she made everyone else happy.

Jake's parents were tired and happy.

His granny was excited and happy.

His aunties and uncles and cousins were smiley and happy. But Jake felt grim.

One night, while his dad put the baby to bed, his mother gave Jake his bath (and let him splash a little bit), and brushed his teeth (and let him squeeze the toothpaste), and snuggled him into bed. It was like old times. She said:

Once upon a time there was just me.

Then I met your dad.

I loved him with a big, big love, as high as the sky.

And I still do.

Then we knew you were coming.

As you grew inside me, the love grew, too.

We loved you with a big, big love, as high as the sky.

We still do.

When we knew that Chloe was coming, guess what happened? The love started growing again.

And it started growing in you, too.

We love her with a big, big love, as high as the sky.

And so do you.

*Then Jake was sleepy **and** happy,
because he knew that it was true.*

The Wild Night

Far away, in a cave in a hillside, there lived a little bear. He was only just beginning to learn about the great, wide world.

One night, when the little bear was curled up ready to sleep, he heard a huge crash!

At the mouth of the cave, he saw a bright flash!

Then there was a whooshing, and a splashing, and it sounded as if the sky was tumbling down.

"Help!" cried the little bear.

But the big bear he lived with came and gave him a cuddle.

"Don't worry," growled the big bear.
"That's just a storm outside."

"But the crashing!" cried the little bear.

"Just thunder," said the big bear.
"But the flashing!" cried the little bear.

"Just lightning," said the big bear.

"But the splashing!" cried the little bear.

"Just rain," replied the big bear, "and the whooshing is just the wind. It's a wild night outside, all right. But do you know what is wonderful about a night like this?"

"No-o-o-o," said the little bear.

"Well, inside our warm cave, there is no crashing, no flashing, and no splashing. There isn't even any whooshing. We are safe and warm, and all that crashing and flashing and splashing and whooshing just makes us feel safer and warmer, doesn't it?"

"It does," said the little bear.
He lay down his head,
and curled up in his bed,
and fell fast asleep.

19

Bedtime Boogie

Stand up tall,
Wave your arms in the air.
Wiggle your bottom
And shake your hair!
Stamp your feet on the ground,
Clap your hands above your head,
Do the Bedtime Boogie
When you're ready for bed!

Stre-e-e-e-etch like a cat
From your head to your toes!
Squiggle like a snake
From your knees to your nose!
Reach to the sky
And touch the floor.
It's the Bedtime Boogie
And it's time for some more!

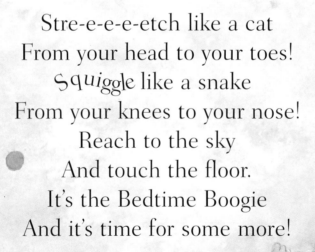

20

Climb into your bed
And make yourself small.
Hug yourself tight
Like a little round ball.
Then stre-e-e-e-etch out your body,
Your fingers and your toes.
You're doing the Bedtime Boogie,
And this is how it goes!

Breathe in to the rhythm
Breathe out to the beat,
Let everything go floppy
From your head to your feet.
As the Bedtime Boogie
Is almost done,
Dance into your dreams,
My dear little one.

Not Yet!

Each night, a little boy's dad would call, "Time to go to sleep now!" "Not yet!" the little boy would shout. "I'm busy!"

Then the boy's dad would come to the door and ask what exactly he was busy doing, and the little boy would mention just one or two things:

"I'm on a pirate ship! We're under attack. I'm worried about our parrot because his feathers are falling out. There's a mermaid under the boat who may be stealing our treasure. I've got a couple of mountains to climb, and a dragon-sighting to investigate before I can go to sleep."

There was always a lot going on in the boy's head. But even pirates with mermaid problems feel sleepy in the end. The little boy often got grumpy and tearful because he wanted badly to go to sleep but he just couldn't stop *thinking* about things.

His dad didn't know what to do with him, until one night, he happened to catch sight of an old bear at the end of the boy's bed.

"Er, does old Button do much these days?" he wondered.

"No, he just sleeps, mostly," said the boy.

"Well, I reckon too much lying around isn't good for a bear," said Dad. "Why not give him some of your trickier missions to handle? It would be good for him, and you'd be able to shut your eyes—just for a while, of course."

The boy could see that the idea had possibilities. In the nights to come, the bear climbed mountains, fought dragons, explored the ocean bed, visited the planet Saturn (twice), and rescued two children from a raging river.

And the boy had enough sleep to see him through just as many adventures . . . during the day.

Lullaby

(Read your child's name where there are dots. Alternate verses are for a girl or a boy to show how easy it is to change just a few words to make it work for any child. If you start with "Once there were two babies", you can read it to twins, too!)

Once there was a baby,
A wriggly, giggly baby,
And everybody loved him,
And . . . . . was his name.

Soon the baby was a toddler.
A walking, talking toddler.
And everybody loved her,
And . . . . . was her name.

24

Sometimes he was angry:
Pouting, *shouting* angry.
But everyone still loved him,
And . . . . . was his name.

Sometimes she was naughty:
Really *very* naughty.
But everyone still loved her,
And . . . . . was her name.

The baby is a big boy now,
A really very big boy now.
But everyone still loves him,
And . . . . . is his name.

Yes, once there was a baby,
A wriggly, giggly baby,
And everybody loves her.
We're very glad she came.

Shhhh!

There was once a little girl who felt cross. She felt so grumpy that she couldn't talk in an ordinary voice. She **shouted**!

"I don't want to eat my dinner!" she shouted, pushing her plate away.

"Then you can't be hungry," said her mother. "Anyway, it's almost time to get undressed."

"I don't want to get undressed!" shouted the little girl, stamping her feet.

"Then I'll do it for you," said her mother. "Your bath is almost ready."

"I don't want to get in the bath!" shouted the little girl, hiding under a towel.

"Then I'll pick you up and put you in," said her mother. "It's almost time for bed."

"I don't want to go to bed!" shouted the little girl, sitting down.

"Then I'll have to carry you like a baby," said her mother. "It's almost time you were asleep."

"I don't want to go to sleep!" shouted the little girl with a fierce face.

"And I don't want to hear any more shouting!" shouted her mother.

"But *you're* shouting," said the little girl.

"I know!" laughed her mother. *"I'm sorry!"*

The little girl laughed. "I'm sorry, too." she said. And soon there were no more shouting sounds, just a little tiny snoring sound.

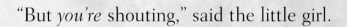

Staying Away

Jack's aunty took him to the park. "We'll keep out of the way until the packing's finished," she said. "Are you very excited about going to the beach?"

Jack kicked at the ground and frowned.

"What's the matter?" asked Aunty.

"What if it rains all the time?" Jack wondered.

"It *might*," Aunty laughed, "but that doesn't matter when you're in your swimming suit."

"What if the food tastes funny?" Jack was still frowning.

"Well, I suppose it *might*, but there will still be ice cream and chips and picnics," said Aunty.

Jack hadn't finished. "What if I go swimming
and a shark comes and bites my toes?"

"It *might*, I suppose," said Aunty seriously. "But those toes
are far too smelly for any self-respecting shark to nibble!"

"What if the hotel is really creepy and I can't get to sleep?"

"It *might* be. But everyone you love best in the world will be
there with you," said Aunty. "Now, I've got a question for you.

What if you just love it?"

At last Jack
smiled. "Well,"
he said, "I *might*."

The New House

Once there was a little girl who went into her old bedroom for the very last time.

Someone who loved her very much came in to say good night. "Tomorrow you'll be in your new room in our new house," he said. "It will be wonderful."

But the little girl sighed. "Goodbye yellow wallpaper," she said. "Goodbye stain on the carpet where I dropped my felt-tip pen and forgot to pick it up. Goodbye view from the window. Goodbye curtains that are too short since they were washed. Goodbye stars on the ceiling that Grandpa put up. Goodbye bracelet that I dropped behind the radiator and no one can get out. Goodbye best bedroom. Everything is going to be strange tomorrow night."

*S*o then there was a little girl who went into her new bedroom for the very first time.

Someone who loved her very much came in to say good night. "How is your new room?" he said. "It looks wonderful."

And the little girl said. "Hello pink wallpaper. Hello new carpet. Hello view from the window. Hello beautiful curtains. Hello stars on the ceiling that Grandpa came specially this afternoon to put up. Hello again toys. Hello again bed."

And the person who loved her said, "You know, I like this house, but the most important thing in it is *you*, and when you put your head on your pillow—like this—and I kiss it and say good night—like this—then this isn't just a *house* any more. It's our *home*, and we're going to be happy here."

"Hello home!" said a sleepy voice. And the new house kept them safe all night long and all the nights ever after.

31

Happy Harry

Alice had a hamster called Harry. He had funny little twitchy whiskers and bright little black eyes. His silky coat was brown and white. He had tiny little toes. He was beautiful.

Alice and Harry were friends for a long time, but one day, when Alice came home from school, a grown-up she loved very much sat down with her and told her that Harry had died. "He was very old for a hamster," he said, "so he curled himself up and went to sleep. Only this time he won't wake up any more."

"You mean I'll never be able to play with him again?"

"No, not now."

"Not ever?"

"Not ever. But ..."

"It isn't fair!" shouted Alice. "I want him back! I'll always clean out his cage if he comes back! I promise!"

"He can't come back," said the grown-up. "I know you feel grumpy and sad. But there are three very important things you must remember."

Alice looked up through her tears.

"Well, first of all, Harry had a happy life. He had his own special cage, and you took care of him so well. He was a lucky little hamster. And second of all, remember that although *you* are feeling sad and angry, Harry isn't. He is all right, and he always will be."

Alice felt a little bit better when she heard that. "And what is the third important thing to remember?" she asked.

"It's Harry!" smiled the grown-up. "We can put a picture of him on your wall, and we can talk about all the funny things he used to do. That way we will never forget him, and he can never really be gone while we still think about him."

And it was true. Harry didn't scamper on his wheel any more, but he lived in Alice's heart, and she knew that he was happy there.

Magic Moon

Gino's dad had to go away for a while. "You'll be fine," he told Gino. "I'll take you to Aunty May's house, and she will look after you until I get back. She really loves you."

But Gino really loved his dad. And his home. And all his toys. And his friends. He didn't want to stay with someone he could hardly remember. And deep inside, so deep he couldn't even think about it, he was worried that his dad wouldn't come back.

"I promise it will be okay," whispered Dad. "I'll be thinking about you every day."

Gino wasn't sure. The big, dark, deep worry was still there. The next day, after work, Dad put Gino's case in the car and drove him to Aunty May's house. It was a long way.

Gino looked out of the window and saw the moon, huge and white and shining. "Goodbye, Moon," he whispered.

It was very late when they arrived. Gino got out of the car, stiff and unhappy. Then he looked up. "Dad, there's a moon here as well!" he said.

"It's the same moon!" Dad laughed.

"It followed me!" Gino gasped. "All the way here!"

Dad looked down. "Yes," he said. "And you know what, it will stay with you every night until I come to get you. And the moon is even more magic than that, because it will follow me as well, to make sure I am okay, too, until I see my own boy again."

Gino suddenly felt strange and solemn and a little bit grown up. The big, dark, deep worry had gone.

So each night, he looked at the moon, and the moon looked at him. And it looked at Dad, too, far away. Until the day came when the moon looked down and smiled to see a boy and his dad —together again.

The Rainbow

*I*t was a dark, miserable day. Allie sat by the window and watched the raindrops running down the glass. Outside, all she could see were wet rooftops and chimneys. "I hate the rain," she said. "There's nothing good about it at all."

"Well, that's not true," said her granny, who was taking care of her. "Plants need rain. Without rain, we couldn't have trees and flowers and grass to play on."

"I can't see any trees and flowers and grass up here," said Allie. She lived high up in a building in the city. "And I couldn't play on the grass today anyway. It's too wet."

"Sweetheart, don't be so miserable," said her granny. "You should try to look on the bright side. Something good always comes out of something bad. I really believe that."

Allie frowned. That was the kind of thing her granny was always saying. She didn't think it was true at all. Because of

the rain, they couldn't go out. Because of the rain, Amir couldn't come to play. Because of the rain, she felt bored and unhappy.

Then, around lunchtime, the rain stopped. The sun came out. And something magical happened to the sky.

"Look at that!" cried Allie. "Look what the sun did!"

Granny grinned. "The sun couldn't do it on its own," she said. "It needed the rain. It's like I said. Something good always comes out of something bad."

Allie smiled, too. That was the kind of thing her granny was always saying. Well, maybe she was right.

A Kiss Like This

Do you like kisses? Augustus did *not*!
When aunts pursed their lips,
he was off like a shot!

"I don't *want* to be smeared
With gluey lipstick!
The smell of their perfume
Makes me feel sick!

And the one with the poodle
(Who wants kisses too)
Has a face that is furry!
She should be in a zoo!

Uncle Christopher slobbers
And smells of old cheese.
Don't make me kiss him,
Or Aunt Sheila, please!"

His mother tried hard
To look stern and severe.
"Augustus, be quiet!
Now just listen here.

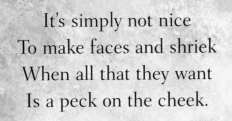

It's simply not nice
To make faces and shriek
When all that they want
Is a peck on the cheek.

But if I am truthful
I have to say this:
They are not always people
I'm eager to kiss.

You shouldn't kiss people
If it doesn't feel right,
If you shake hands instead
They will think you're polite."

That night at bedtime,
Augustus lay down
And his mother came in
With a smile *and* a frown.

"Good night, Gus," she said,
And held out her hand,
But Augustus jumped up.
"No, you don't understand!

Some kisses are awful, but yours are the best!
And a kiss like this . . . mmmm . . . is worth all the rest!"

Our Princess

One night, our mother arranged for Annie from next door to take care of us while she went to a party. We *did* **not** think that was right.

While our mother went to get dressed,
Annie put us in the bath.

We said:

"It isn't fair! Why can't we go to the party too?"

"Mothers don't need to go to parties. We do!"

"We don't like it when she isn't here."

"She should be taking care of *us*!"

"What if we get scared in the night?"

40

Annie said:

"It is a party for grown-ups."

"Your mother works hard every day.
Of course she needs to go to a party!"

"I am here to look after you.
Your mother would *never* leave you alone.
She'll come to say good night before she goes."

Annie tucked us into our beds. There was a rustle
at the door. In came someone with glittery jewels
in her ears and around her neck. And a dress that
went ***woosh! swoosh!*** when she walked.
And sparkly, pointy shoes. And when she leaned
over us to say good night, she smelled ***wonderful!***

We said:

"*Wow!* We didn't know you
were a **princess!**
Have a great time!"

After all, even if mothers
shouldn't go to parties,
princesses
really **should!**

Naughty or Not?

Robert-John did naughty things every day.
Which was the naughtiest? Can you say?

He put peanut butter in his little sister's shoes.

He scared his granny with monster shouts.

He drew on the wall (and signed his name).

Rob

He bounced on his bed—and broke it!

He walked through mud in his best shoes.

He made his mother cry.

Robert-John tried to do better.

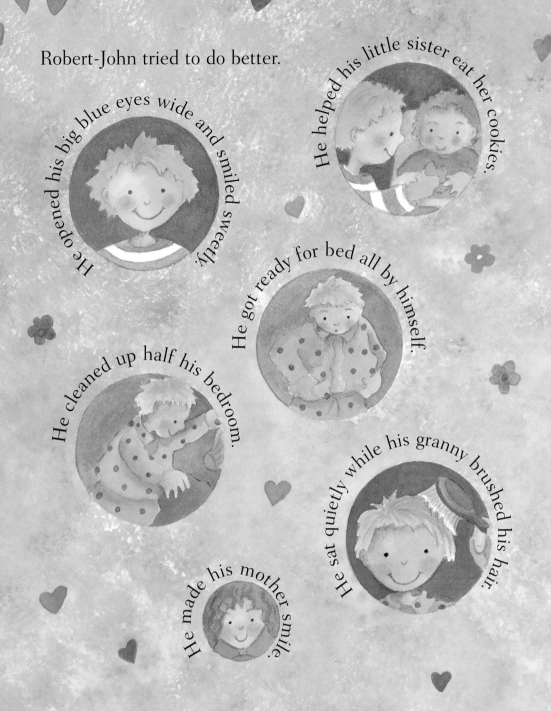

He opened his big blue eyes wide and smiled sweetly.

He helped his little sister eat her cookies.

He got ready for bed all by himself.

He cleaned up half his bedroom.

He sat quietly while his granny brushed his hair.

He made his mother smile.

Did he succeed? What do you say?
And what was the best thing
that YOU did today?

The Good Night

There was once a princess who decided she didn't like night-time. "Take it away!" she cried. "From now on, there will only be day!"

"My dear!" The king tried to protest. He didn't think it was *possible* to take away the night.

An old woman stepped forward. She wore a purple cloak and had a round, smiling face. "I can do what the princess wishes," she said, "if she is *really* sure."

"I said so, didn't I?" the princess rudely replied.

So the old woman went outside and waited. When the shadows across the lawns were as dark and purple as her cloak, she knelt down and began to roll up the dark like a carpet. It took a long time, for the dark was everywhere.

44

When she had finished, it was daytime wherever you looked. The princess smiled. For a whole year, there was only day. Everything was always bright and busy.

Then, one day, in a high turret of the castle, the princess opened an old cupboard and found . . . a little piece of darkness left inside. It was inky blue and soft and peaceful. It felt so calm and quiet and *right* that the princess climbed inside and went to sleep.

When she woke up, she went to find the only person who could help.

"There's no need to say anything," said the old woman. "I know what you want. Perhaps you can help me."

Together, the two unrolled the night, so that it covered everything again. They stood under the stars and smiled.

"Good night, my dear," said the old woman.

"Good night," said the princess. "It really is, isn't it?"

"Oh yes," the old woman said. "The night is very good indeed."

The Sleepy Sea

Milly couldn't sleep. "I've got too many thoughts," she said. "My head is full of them. They won't go away."

Someone who loved Milly very much said, "Are your thoughts like butterflies, flitting lightly here and there?"

"A little bit," said Milly.

"Or are they like birds, fluttering and singing and hopping from branch to branch?"

"Not very much like birds," said Milly.

"Maybe your thoughts are like bright little fish, flashing here and there. Do they dart about, and swim and swoop, silently and smoothly in the warm, blue sea?"

"Yes," said Milly. "That's just what they're like. And they never stay still! Not even for a second!"

Then the person who loved her smiled and said, "That's because the sea is never still. Your thoughts are never still either. But when you go to sleep, you need them to be more peaceful. Shut your eyes. I'll tell you what happens."

So Milly shut her eyes and imagined a sunny sea, full of quick little fish.

She heard a quiet voice. "Look," it said. "The sun is sliding down below the sea, turning everything to gold. Now it is gone, and the water is becoming darker, deep blue under the shining moon and stars. The little fish look silver now, and as the waves roll gently across the water, the fish sway softly backwards and forwards, rocking in the warm arms of the sea. Listen, can you hear your breathing? It's like the sound of the sighing sea."

Milly drifted into sleep, and all night long, the warm sea soothed her bright little fish and kept them as still as fish or thoughts can be—until morning.

Christmas Eve

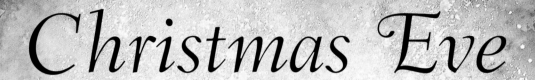

One Christmas, Granny came to stay. She tucked Emily into bed and read her a story. But Emily just couldn't keep still. She bounced up and said, "I'm too excited to sleep!"

Granny sighed. "Just shut your eyes and think of something wonderful."

"I am!" cried Emily. "I'm thinking of presents!"

"Oh, I can think of something better than that," said Granny. "And more exciting, too."

"More exciting than presents?"

"Yes," said Granny firmly. "Haven't you ever flown with the reindeer? Now shut your eyes. Imagine you are at the North Pole. It's cold there, remember. You'll need your warm blanket. Look! There's Santa's sleigh, waiting for him.

48

The reindeer are stamping. They want to be off. Listen!
Their bells are jingling. Quick! Climb into the back of the
sleigh and hide. Oh, here comes Santa! Keep very still!
Breathe very quietly! The sleigh is starting to move. It's
swishing across the snow! It's going faster and faster! It's
taking off! Oooooh! You're flying through the sky! The stars
are twinkling, the sleigh bells are jingling. It's the most
wonderful feeling. Keep very still. Now, where is the
sleigh going? Over forests and rivers. Over hills
and seas. Look, there are rooftops far below!"

Granny's voice was soft and warm.
She described the long, long journey.
The sleigh was heading for a
certain house. A house
Emily knew well!

Granny looked down at Emily.
She was fast asleep.
She didn't even hear
the sleigh bells jingling
just outside her window...

The Best Bed

Once there was a little girl who would **not** stay in her own bed. In the middle of the night her parents would hear little footsteps on the floor, and a bashing and a crashing as she flung back their door.

One day, her very sleepy dad couldn't stand it any more. "Don't you know," he said, "that every creature in the world has its own bed? I know a little elephant who has a nice bed on the ground beside a scrubby bush in Africa. And I know a parrot who sleeps on a special branch just above. I know a pony with a super stable, full of warm straw. And there's a little girl I know, not very far from here, who has a beautiful princess bed that **she should stay in!**"

"Why?" asked the little girl.

"Because," her dad replied, "if one person . . . just one person . . . starts moving about in the middle of the night, there could be terrible trouble. Suppose that pony suddenly realizes someone isn't sleeping in her beautiful princess bed? He might decide to move in himself, hoofs and all! And what if the parrot decides to sleep on the ground beside a scrubby bush? Where can that baby elephant sleep? Well, it's obvious. He will have to sleep on the special branch above. And I think that might be very bad news for the parrot!"

The little girl thought about this. She could see it made sense. So she went to sleep in her princess bed, and she stayed there all night long. (And the parrot was fine, too.)

Lost and Found

One night, when Giles went to bed, his mother came and sat next to him. "I want to tell you about my extraordinary day," she said. Giles was surprised. It had been a very ordinary day, he thought.

"Today," his mother began, "has been the worst day of my life. Do you remember this morning, when we went to the supermarket? You thought it would be funny to run away and hide."

"I didn't go far," said Giles.

"Oh, sweetheart, it's such a big store. I hunted everywhere for you, but I couldn't find you. I asked everyone if they had seen you. They hadn't, but they helped me to look. Then someone went to tell the manager, and he made sure that lots of people helped me."

"Everyone looking for me!" grinned Giles.
But his mother wasn't smiling.

"I was so afraid," she said.
"I kept remembering your happy
little face, and I started to cry.
I thought I might never see you
again, and I couldn't bear it."

"Don't cry now, Mama," said Giles,
because her face was looking funny.

"Then the manager himself found you near the chocolate,"
said his mother, "and he brought you over to me.
I was happy and angry all at the same time."

"I won't do it any more," said Giles.

"That's good," his mother whispered. "We'll both remember
today. The little person I love best in all the world came
back to me. So although it was the worst day I've ever
known, it was the very best day ever, too."

Staying Safe

Ian loved to stay with his granny. But at night, all alone in his big bed, he felt very small.

"Sweet dreams!" said Granny. "See you in the morning!"

Ian tried to smile. "What's the matter?" asked Granny.

"Dreams," said Ian in a small voice. "Sometimes."

"Ah, sometimes there are scary things?" Granny seemed to know all about it. "I knew a little girl once," she said, "who had very exciting dreams. In her dreams she climbed dragon-infested mountains and swam crocodile-infested rivers and sailed shark-infested seas. She had a wonderful time! It was great!" Granny's face had a dreamy, faraway look. "But didn't the dragons and the crocodiles and the sharks . . . you know?" asked Ian.

"Good gracious, no!" laughed Granny. "Of course not. She had a special shield. Not like knights of old, but a glow around her that meant dragons and crocodiles and sharks and anything else that might make dreams scary couldn't ever hurt her. She had it because lots of people loved her very much. The love protected her and kept her safe."

Ian didn't like to ask, but Granny smiled.

"Of course, you've got it too!" she cried. "Aren't you the most wonderful, most special, most loved boy in the whole wide world?"

Well, yes, Ian knew that it was true, so he set off happily into his dreams and was safe all night long.

And … just a minute! Aren't you the most wonderful, most special, most loved boy (or girl!) in the whole wide world, too? Well, that means you have the special shield, too. I bet you just can't wait to get to sleep. Sweet dreams!

Whose Bed?

Once there was a little girl who always had
something to say . . . especially at bedtime!
One night, her babysitter told her it was time
for bed. But Lucy shouted:

"I never, ever go to bed
Without Mr. Benjamin Bingle Ted."

So Mr. Benjamin Bingle Ted
Joined little Lucy in the bed.

Then, "Wait a minute!" Lucy cried,
"I need Mrs. Bunny by my side!"

So Mrs. Bunny went in, too,
And her children—Pinky, Pumpkin and Boo.

"Wait! I'm not ready to go to sleep!
I need Humpty and Cinders and Little Bo-Peep!"

So Humpty and Cinders and Little Bo-Peep
Were squeezed into bed so that Lucy could sleep.

"And I need Noah and all of his crew,"
Lucy said, "and all the animals, too."

The babysitter did her best.
She tucked in Noah and all the rest.

But . . .

"Wait!" called Lucy. "Can't you see?
There isn't any room for me!"

The toys were taken out of bed
And Lucy lay down her sleepy head.

"Good night!" The babysitter hurried away . . .
Before Lucy found something else to say!

Birthday Bunny

Benny Bunny was always bouncy, but one night he was extra-super-specially bouncy. You see, he knew that next day was his birthday.

"I can't sleep!" cried Benny.
"I'm too excited!"
He bounced out of
his bed and down the stairs.

"Back to bed, young bunny!"
called his dad.

Boiiing!

Boiiing!

"I'm too excited!"
shouted Benny.

"Look out!" yelled Dad.

"I feel as if I've got squiggly
things in my tummy!"
chortled Benny.

Boiiing!

"Benny!" Dad got bounced on!
He was not a happy bunny.

"Sorry!" said Benny, but he still couldn't keep still. Nothing his mother or father said would make him go back to bed.

"Well, *we're* going to bed,"
said his parents at last.
"If you can't go to sleep,
you'll just have to stay up,
Benny. See you in the morning!"

Boiing!

Benny bounced all night long. But when the sun slipped up over the windowsill in the morning, he couldn't keep his eyes open any longer. When Mr. and Mrs. Bunny came down, they found a little bunny sleeping under the kitchen table.

Benny slept . . . and slept . . . and slept. His friends came to his party, but he was still asleep. When at last he woke up, it was morning. "It's my birthday!" yelled Benny Bunny.

Dad shook his head. "That was yesterday, Benny."

Poor Benny! Of course, he opened his presents,
and his friends came over for a *second* party,
but it wasn't the same. When it's time for *your*
birthday, make sure you go to sleep, won't you?
You have to wait a whole year for the next one!

59

Sleepy Monkeys

Deep in the jungle lived two little monkeys, Chuckles and Jimble. They shared a huge tree with their parents, a snake, several parrots, two lizards and a family of frogs, but the monkeys had their own branch, of course.

The trouble started when Chuckles' and Jimble's baby sister was born. "Now boys," said their dad, "you are old enough to have your own branch. You can share that big leafy part at the end."

Chuckles and Jimble were pleased to have their own branch at last. They settled down to sleep that night feeling very grown up.

But pretty soon that branch began to bounce . . . and to wobble . . . and to jiggle. Those monkey boys had realized that out of sight of their parents they could have fun instead of going to sleep.

"Stop that right now!" called Dad.
"Don't think I can't feel that bouncing!"

The monkeys were still for a minute,
then the end of the branch started
to move suspiciously again.

"You're jiggling the whole tree!" called Dad.
"If you're not careful, you'll wake everybody up.
Chuck! Jim! Go to sleep!"

I wish I could say that those monkey boys
curled up and closed their eyes. But I can't.
They didn't listen to their father.

Next morning, Mr. Monkey swung along to the end of the
branch and found no naughty monkeys at all . . . but one
fat and sleepy snake!

Do you think the snake
had a midnight snack?
Or did he send those
monkeys to another
branch, where they
couldn't wake anyone
up? Do *you* know any
naughty monkeys who
don't go straight to sleep?

61

Get Up Now!

Once upon a time there was a lazy farmer. He knew he should get up early to start his work, but he didn't like to leave his bed. One morning, his animals gave him a surprise.

Drriiiing!

The farmer's alarm clock rang early as usual. The farmer turned it off and went back to sleep.

Clomp! Clomp! Moo!

Someone very large was coming up the stairs and into the bedroom! "It's time I was milked!" bellowed Clarice the cow.

The farmer shut his eyes tighter.

Thud! Thud! Snuffle!

Two fat, pink animals were scrambling up the stairs and across the room! "It's time for our breakfast!" snorted Polly and Wally the pigs.

The farmer snored on.

Clatter! Clatter! Baa!

Three woolly white creatures hopped up the stairs and bumped into the bed! "We need to be taken to the hillside!" bleated Daisy and Dolly and Arthur the sheep.

"Mmmnnnhmmph!" muttered the farmer.

Scritch! Scratch! Cluck!

Four angry birds fluttered up the stairs. Three landed on the farmer's head! "We want our food!" squawked Henny, Penny, Jenny and Josie the hens.

Clatter! Clatter! Baa!

The farmer sat up, still with three hens on his head, and looked around his room. He hadn't gone out to the farm, but the farm had come to him!

After that, the farmer was up bright and early every morning. Are you?

63

Noisy Toys

S ita's dad looked round the door.
"It's time to go to sleep now," he said.
"No more noise, please!"

Sita grinned. "I don't make noise!
It isn't me. It's my naughty toys!"

The clown goes bing!
The bus goes ting!
The fairy shakes her bell
With a ting-a-ling-ling!

"Come on, Sita," her dad said.
"You are the noisy one. Time for bed!"

Sita giggled. "I don't make noise!
It isn't me. It's my naughty toys!"

The drum goes bang!
The cymbal goes crash!
The cars whiz around
And go brrrm! vrrrrm! bash!

Dad looked angry and shook his head.
"You shouldn't tell fibs like that," he said.

At last sleepy Sita stopped making noise.
She climbed into bed and left her toys.

But two minutes later . . .

The clown went bing!
The bus went ting!
The fairy shook her bell
With a ting-a-ling-ling!

The drum went bang!
The cymbal went crash!
The cars whizzed around
And went brrrm! vrrrrm! bash!

Sita couldn't stop the terrible noise.
If only she hadn't blamed her toys!

Then Sita told Dad what really happened before,
And those toys were not noisy any more.

The Scary Place

Ellie didn't want to go to sleep. She didn't know why. She just didn't. But someone who loved her very much had an idea.

"It's your first day at preschool tomorrow, isn't it?" the special person asked. "Maybe you're worried that it's a scary place? It isn't, you know. Don't you remember when we went to see it? Do you know what I always do if I have to go to a scary place?"

"No," mumbled Ellie.

"Well, I go there in my head first," said the person who loved her more than the moon and stars.

Ellie frowned. "How?"

"I shut my eyes. You do it, too. That's right. Now, let's put our coats on. Hey, you've got *my* coat! This one won't fit me!"

Ellie giggled.

"OK, now here we go. We'll go in the car. Let me help with your seat belt. All right? It's not far."

Before Ellie had a chance to be scared, her special driver was saying, "We're here! Come on!" And someone with a very smiley face was saying, "Ellie! How lovely to see you! Come and put your coat here. Look, we've put your name on your peg!"

And Ellie saw some wonderful toys, and a lot of children who looked as if they really wanted to be friends. But before she was ready, someone she loved more than chocolate and ice cream said, "Time to go home now! Did you have a nice time?" And Ellie said, "Already?" But she got in the car and came home like a good girl.

Then the person who loved her said, "You know what? It's going to be just as much fun tomorrow, when you *really* go."

Ellie said, "I want to go to sleep *right now*!" And she did.

The Dreamboat

Sam was sad. His Dad worked on a huge ocean liner, sailing around the world all year long. When he came home, it was a very special time. Sam loved to hear stories of all the places Dad had visited. But now it was time for Dad to go again.

Sam lay in his bed and faced the wall.

"Not even going to say goodbye?" asked his dad.

Sam didn't say a word. He shut his eyes tight so that the tears wouldn't come out. But when Dad kissed him and quietly walked towards the door, he held out his arms.

"I wish you didn't have to go!
I wish I could go too!
I wish I could see all the places you see!"

Dad smiled and came back. "That's a lot of wishes, pal. I'm afraid I do have to go. You know that. But there is something you can do about the other wishes."

Sam looked up and wiped his face.

"When I was a boy," said Dad, "I longed to go to sea.
I knew it would be years and years before I could.
But every night, when I shut my eyes, I imagined all the
places I wanted to see. I called it sailing on my dreamboat."

"Did it work?" asked Sam doubtfully.

"Did it work? I went around the world six times.
And look what I do for a living now!
Of course it works! I'm ready to sail. Are you?"

"Aye, aye, Cap'n!" Sam smiled,
shutting his eyes. "I'll tell you all
about it when you get back."

"I can't wait," whispered Dad.

Magic Hugs

Once there was a little bear called Tig. He was excited when he heard he was going to stay with his cousins the Biffle boys. He knew he would have fun. But when he went to bed that first night in the Biffle house, Tig felt a funny feeling in his tummy.

"Good night, Tig," said his Aunty. "Sweet dreams!"

"Good night!" said Tig, in a small, sad voice.

Aunty put her head on one side. "Feeling homesick, Tig?" she asked. "Missing your folks at home?"

Tig nodded. He couldn't explain that bedtimes were a special time, when his big, cuddly mother and his even bigger, cuddly dad, and his three cuddly little sisters piled onto his bed and gave him a huge family hug.

Aunty sat down beside the little bear. "Do you know what I do?" she asked. "My very biggest boy has left home now. My mother and father live faraway in the mountains. My little sister, who has cubs of her own, lives overseas. But every night, before I go to sleep, I give them a magic hug."

"A magic hug?" Tig snuggled a little closer to his aunty.

"Yes, I'll tell you how to do it. You shut your eyes, and one by one you think of all the people you love who are far away. And when you've got them all together, you put a smile around them instead of your arms. A great big smile that will keep them safe until you see them again. And do you know what else I think? I'm pretty sure that at just exactly the same moment you're giving your folks a magic hug, they're giving you one right back."

So Tig shut his eyes. He thought of his mother and his dad and his sisters. Then he put a smile right around them. And as he drifted off to sleep, still smiling, he was sure he could feel big furry arms giving him a great big magic family hug, too.

Which Dream?

Close your eyes,
If you want a surprise.
Wave your finger in the air,
Let it land anywhere.
If the dream's not right, then
Try all over again!

You are a prince or princess in a beautiful castle...

You are a clown with a huge red nose...

You are a crocodile...

You are a pirate, sailing away...

You are a mermaid under the sea...

You have a pony called Midnight Star...

Everything you touch becomes a rainbow...

Your grandma has a magic wand...

When you sing, everyone starts to dance...

Your bed is a space rocket, heading for the stars......

You are a mouse...

All your toys can talk to you...

You can fly...

You're as tall as a tree...

73

All Asleep!

Five little children got ready for bed,
But did they shut their eyes? No!
"We're not sleepy!" they said.

One started bouncing, hopping and jumping,
Leaping and bumping all over his bed.
His legs got wobbly, tired and wobbly,
But he wouldn't give in. "I'm not sleepy!" he said.

One started singing, chanting and humming,
Banging and strumming all over her bed.
Her voice got fainter, tired and fainter,
But she wouldn't give in. "I'm not sleepy!" she said.

One started laughing, chortling and giggling,
Wriggling and squiggling all over his bed.
His tummy got achey, tired and achey,
But he wouldn't give in. "I'm not sleepy!" he said.

One started swaying, spinning and dancing,
Twirling and prancing all over her bed.
Her arms felt heavy, tired and heavy,
But she wouldn't give in. "I'm not sleepy!" she said.

One was playing pirates, swashing and buckling,
Yo-ho-ho-ing and chuckling all over his bed.
His eyelids were drooping, tired and drooping,
But he wouldn't give in. "I'm not sleepy!" he said.

But the bouncer and singer, giggler and spinner,
And even the pirate soon crawled into bed.
They all felt sleepy, tired and sleepy,
And they had to give in. "Zzzzzzzzz!" they said.

Sleeping Well

Once there was a little tiny girl called Poppy. She wished with all her heart that she could be bigger. One night, she told her granny that she didn't want to go to sleep.

"Why not?" Granny asked.

"I'm busy," said Poppy. She sat very still with a serious look on her face.

"Busy doing what?"

"I'm growing," said Poppy. "I need to concentrate. I haven't got time to sleep."

Granny smiled. "Oh, Poppy," she said, "you *have* to go to sleep if you are going to grow up to be a big girl!"

Poppy knew that Granny was clever as well as cuddly. She put her head on one side to listen.

"At night," said Granny, "just as much happens as during the day."

"What happens?" asked Poppy.

"Everything!" Granny grinned.
"Your heart keeps beating.
Your body keeps breathing.
Your tummy keeps dealing with your dinner.
And most of all, you keep growing.
Your hair keeps growing.
Your nails keep growing.
All of you keeps on growing, so that every morning you are bigger and better and more beautiful than you were the day before. Though I really don't see how you *could* be more beautiful than you are today."

And Granny, that very clever, cuddly Granny, was right. Every night, the world keeps turning, and the stars keep shining, and Poppy keeps growing—and so do you!

And tomorrow morning, you will be bigger and better and more beautiful than you are today. Though I really don't see how you **could** *be more beautiful than you are today.*

Sleep well!

Scary Shadows

One night, Emma asked her Dad to leave the light on. Not the little light near her bed, but the big, bright light in the middle of the ceiling.

"You'll never be able to get to sleep with that on," said Dad. "What's the matter?"

"I'm scared," said Emma.

"Scared? My big beautiful girl in her pretty bed? What are you scared of?" asked Dad.

"I can't tell you." Emma opened her eyes wide to show how scared she was.

"Would it help if you whispered?" asked Dad. He knew that sometimes scary things just can't be said out loud.

Emma whispered. "There are s-s-s-scary sh-sh-sh-shadows!"

Dad looked serious. "There's only one thing to do about
that," he said. "We need to go on a scary shadow hunt.
You stay here. I'll get my equipment."

Dad came back with his big torch from the garage.
"Hold my hand," he said. "We'll do this together."

Then Dad turned off the big light.
The shadow-hunters crept around the room,
shining the torch into every corner.

"What are we doing?" whispered Emma.

"We're scaring the scary shadows," said Dad.
"Look! No shadows here, no shadows there!
Wait a minute! That *is* a scary shadow. Aaaagh!"

"That's my shadow, Dad!" Emma laughed.
"That's not scary!"

Then Dad and Emma sat on the
bed and made scary shadows and
funny shadows on the wall with
their hands, and they laughed
so much that Emma forgot to
be scared—and the shadows
forgot to be scary.

Choosing a Story